Look Doogie Bowser, I just lost a tooth.

Where shall I keep it?

In my
coloring
book.

I know. I will put it in my toy box.

How about in my kangaroo's pouch?

I will put my tooth in my slipper.

I know. I will put my tooth under my pillow.

I cannot wait until I lose another tooth.